RUDOLPH W. GIULIANI

AMERICA'S MAYOR

BY ELEANOR FREMONT

ALADDIN PAPERBACKS
New York   London   Toronto   Sydney   Singapore

First Aladdin Paperbacks edition May 2002

Text copyright © 2002 by Ellen Weiss

ALADDIN PAPERBACKS
An imprint of Simon & Schuster
Children's Publishing Division
1230 Avenue of the Americas
New York, NY 10020

Designed by Sammy Yuen Jr.
The text of this book was set in 12pt Palatino.

Printed in the United States of America
2 4 6 8 10 9 7 5 3 1

Library of Congress Control Number 2001012345

ISBN 0-689-85423-4

J 92

★ INTRODUCTION ★

Rudy. In New York, New York, the name stands alone. It is unnecessary to add a last name, and from here on in, perhaps it always will be. It is a name that runs like an electric charge through the granite canyons of the city, stirring up feelings on every block, in every neighborhood, in each of the five boroughs that make up the great metropolis. And since September 11, 2001, it has been known across the United States and all around the globe. Rudolph Giuliani, the 107th mayor of New York, has become, in a phrase frequently used during the fall of 2001, the mayor of America. And when *Time* magazine chose him in December to be its "Man of the Year," it called him "The Mayor of the World."

Before September 11, Rudy was an extremely controversial mayor who was just about to end his final term at City Hall. Like the widely held image of the town he loved and led, he was tough, brash, strong-minded, and scrappy, but never dull. There was nothing wishy-washy about Rudy. He seemed always to be in a war of words with somebody or other. Under Rudy, the crime rate in the city was lower than it had been in decades, but his methods were severe. He was an unabashed Yankees fan, and didn't care who knew it. Some New Yorkers adored him, some couldn't stand him. Outside the city he was not much better known than any other big-city mayor.

But on that crisp, clear, terrible fall day in September, after the twin towers of the World Trade Center blew apart, New Yorkers became acquainted with a side of Rudy Giuliani they had never seen. Suddenly they were in the presence of a magnificent wartime leader. He was fearless, and he made them less afraid. He told them the truth, and they found they could handle it. He was calm, and he made them feel less jangled. He told them that they could be better and stronger people as a result of this horrible trauma—and maybe, just for a while, they became better and stronger people.

Who is this man of a thousand contradictions? Why are there so many sides to Rudy Giuliani? And what were the forces that made him into the mayor who could be so tough and so tender, so cantankerous and yet so compassionate? Were the seeds of the new crisis-born leader always inside the feisty mayor New Yorkers thought they knew so well?

The answer begins, as it must, at the beginning—on May 28, 1944.

CHAPTER ONE

Rudolph William Louis Giuliani was born on a Sunday, to parents who had hoped and prayed for a baby for so long that when he finally showed up, they felt he was a gift straight from God.

Rudy's father, Harold, was deliriously happy. As soon as he got the news of the baby's birth he ran up and down his block in Brooklyn, passing out cigars at every house and shouting that his wife, Helen, had given birth to a boy. The infant was named after Harold's father, Rodolpho.

The new baby was brought home to the embrace of a large, lively family. His parents lived at 419 Hawthorne Street, in a two-family house owned by Helen's mother, Adelina. The brick house was just like all the others on the street, and in fact they were all connected together at the sides. Each house had an iron gate out front, and steps leading up to the front door. Rudy and his family lived with his grandmother in a six-room apartment on the second floor. His grandmother cooked huge meals for them all, and took care of Rudy a lot of the time. The new baby was not a good sleeper. Often he was awake all night, and Adelina stayed up with him.

In the apartment downstairs lived Harold's brother William, who happened to be married to Helen's sister Olga. It was no accident that the two pairs of brothers and sisters were married: William and Olga had met at Harold and Helen's wedding in 1936. William was a detective with the New York City Police Department in Brooklyn. He and Olga had two daughters, Evangeline and Joan Ellen, who loved taking care of and playing with little Rudy.

And three doors down the street lived Helen's sister Fanny and her husband John. They had two children as well, Assunta and Frederick. Assunta was fourteen years older than Rudy and remembers teaching Helen to change the baby's first diaper.

Rudy's extended family went on and on. Harold and Helen each had several brothers and sisters, and so Rudy had an enormous cast of cousins, aunts, and uncles. There were two grandmothers, each of whom had lost her husband at an early age. Both of them were round, giving, and loving.

Rudy's father's family, the Giulianis, were from northern Italy. Harold's father, Rodolpho, had come to America in the 1880s. He had sailed to New York from Tuscany, a beautiful area near the city of Florence. He was a tailor, and his wife, Evangelina, was a seamstress who could make beautiful dresses. They settled in the Manhattan neighborhood of East Harlem, which had a large Italian-American population, and had five children together. Rodolpho was an opera lover who loved to sing along with records, but he had a stubborn and stormy disposition.

As many immigrants did, Evangelina worked outside the home, toiling for long, hard hours in a garment factory. Rodolpho stayed home, made suits on his sewing machine, and tended the children. Harold, the oldest child, was often sent out to deliver finished suits to customers. When he dawdled, his father punished him harshly.

By the time he was fifteen years old, he had dropped out of high school. There was nothing else to do but get into trouble, and get into trouble he did. He was arrested for burglary soon after he dropped out, but was sentenced only to probation, which meant that if he did nothing else wrong he would not have to do time in jail. A big, powerful man with enormous hands, he tried being a professional fighter, but his eyes were too bad. He trained for work as a plumber's helper, but there was very little work available.

★ ★ ★

While Harold was growing up in Manhattan's East Harlem, Helen was being raised in Brooklyn. Her mother, Adelina, was used to hard work. Adelina had come to America in 1884, when she was two years old. By the time she was thirteen, Adelina's mother had died, leaving her to care for her younger brother and sister. When she was twenty-one, she met a man named Luigi D'Avanzo. He had come from the same region of southern Italy that she had. After they got married, they bought a house in Brooklyn and raised seven children there.

Harold and Helen first met at a party around the year 1930. This was the beginning of a rough period in American history: the Great Depression. The stock market had crashed in 1929, and almost everyone was having trouble making a living. Nobody had enough money, and basics like food and clothing were scarce. Luxuries, like toys for children or fancy clothing and jewelry, were totally beyond the reach of most people. Harold and Helen went on the kind of dates most people did in those hard times, taking walks or having picnics in the park.

Helen was quiet, polite, and reserved—everything that Harold was not. She had skipped two grades in school, and graduated at sixteen, which was also the year in which her father died. Her five older brothers did not approve of Helen's new beau and tried to talk her out of seeing him. Harold's awful temper did not help matters. He was always getting into fights with men he felt were disrespecting Helen or even other women on the street.

In 1934 Harold really got into trouble. He had been unable to find work, and he was at the end of his rope. He and a friend followed a milkman into an apartment building. The milkman was collecting money for his deliveries that day. They cornered the man in a stairwell, threatened him with a gun, and robbed him of $128.82.

Harold was arrested and sentenced to two to five years at Sing Sing State Prison in upstate New York. Sing Sing is one of the country's most notoriously unpleasant prisons, a dark brown fortress that still broods over the Hudson River.

After serving sixteen months at Sing Sing, Harold was released on parole. If he stayed out of trouble and kept in touch with his parole officer, he was finished with prison. He had paid back his debt to society.

★CHAPTER TWO★

A year later Helen D'Avanzo married Harold. A couple of years later they moved to the Hawthorne Street house in Brooklyn, and soon after that, Harold finished his parole. He was truly a free man now, ready to move on with his life and hoping to be a father.

Life in Brooklyn, as well as in the rest of the country, was not easy. The country had recovered from the trauma of the Depression, but now there was a new trauma: World War II. The evil of the Nazis had infected almost every corner of the globe, until the conflict engulfed a reluctant United States when the Japanese attacked Pearl Harbor in 1941. Across America every family that had a young man who could fight in the war had to watch him go off, not knowing if he would come back or not. One of Harold's brothers was serving in the Pacific. The other young men remained in New York, since they were already in uniform as firemen or policemen, or were too young to serve. Because he had done time in prison, Harold was not eligible to serve in the armed forces.

Harold and Helen wanted badly to have a baby, but parenthood was not something that came easily to them. Their first pregnancy had ended in a miscarriage. It was not until six years after their marriage that Rudy was born. Helen was thirty-five years old. At that time, thirty-five was very late to have a baby. That was why Rudy was treated as "the little prince," in the words of some of their relatives.

Rudy was a wartime baby, and on the home front, scarcity was the watchword. Most of the country's resources were channeled into the war effort. People were issued books of ration coupons for everything from coffee to sugar to gasoline. People across the country were encouraged to grow their own vegetables in "victory gardens." Nylon stockings for women were nonexistent because all the nylon went into making parachutes for soldiers, so women took to putting makeup on their legs to look as if they had stockings on. Shoes were rationed, and when a family had a growing child, family members often had to chip in their shoe coupons so the little ones could be kept in shoes that fit.

Helen devoted all her time to caring for her son. She was determined to give him every bit of enrichment she could. As he got older she liked to read aloud to him from history books and biographies. Politics and history were always subjects of lively dinnertime conversation in the Giuliani household. And, of course, all of America had just gotten a hard-won education in politics and history. The Second World War ended in 1945, and final estimates of the worldwide death toll from the war range from forty to fifty million people.

The Depression and the war years shaped the characters of a whole generation of Americans. Children who were born during this period often learned uncompromising values from their parents, who had had to learn to live through years of fear, uncertainty, and harsh circumstances. The lessons that got passed along tended to revolve around being tough in the face of hardship, pitching in when others needed help, making do with little, and—perhaps most of all—not complaining. All these were values that Rudy learned early and took with him into adulthood.

When he was five, Rudy was sent to kindergarten

at Saint Francis of Assisi Catholic school. It was a strict place where the teachers, some of them priests, were not afraid to box ears and smack wrists if they felt a child needed discipline. By some accounts, Rudy was a wiggly child, always in motion, and was often on the receiving end of this discipline.

While Helen was seeing to the development of young Rudy's mind, her husband was working on toughening the boy up. When Rudy was just two years old, Harold gave him a tiny pair of boxing gloves so he could learn to defend himself. And then, a couple of years later, Harold did something that ended up meaning that Rudy would really need to defend himself.

Brooklyn, in those days, was mad for the Brooklyn Dodgers. The team played in Ebbets Field, which was only a ten-minute walk from the Giulianis' house. Being a fan of the Dodgers was a matter of pride and honor for Brooklynites. Harold didn't care about the Dodgers, though. He had come from East Harlem, a stone's throw from Yankee Stadium, and he was a Yankees fan through and through. Of course there was no question that his son would be too. Rudy played on a neighborhood Little League team and loved baseball. One day Harold bought his son a little Yankees uniform and sent Rudy out into the streets with it on. Of course, the neighborhood kids were outraged by this provocation. In a story Rudy has often told, he came within an inch of disaster. In a campaign commercial that ran when he was running for mayor in 1993, Rudy recalled, "The first thing they did was throw me in the mud. I kept telling them, 'I'm a Yankee fan. I'm gonna stay a Yankee fan.'" The way the story goes, the other kids improvised a noose and managed to get it around Rudy's neck. The only thing that saved the little boy was his grandmother Adelina who came flying out of the house, screeching at the top of her lungs and scaring the gang away. "To my father," Rudy recalled, "it was a joke." He'd put a Yankees uniform on his son, and it would annoy all his relatives and neighbors and provide lots of amusement. "But to me," said Rudy, "it was like being a martyr: I'm not gonna give up my religion. You're not gonna change me." If it was Harold's aim to make Rudy tougher and more stubborn, he may very well have succeeded.

Just as Helen considered it her job to teach Rudy about history and its great leaders, Harold was bent on giving his son a moral education, so that Rudy would not stray onto the same path his father had. He was constantly admonishing the boy: Don't take anything that's not yours. Don't steal. Don't lie. Never lie, never steal.

As an adult, Rudy Giuliani remembers these lessons well. When he was young, he could never understand why his father was telling him these things. Rudy wasn't going to steal anything, so why was his father always repeating these warnings?

For most of his life Rudy knew very little about his father's dark secret. Even after he became mayor, he says, the details were shadowy. At home no one ever discussed Harold's time in prison. It was not until Rudy's biographer, a reporter named Wayne Barrett, uncovered documents and witnesses that filled in the gaps that Rudy knew the full story. And once he knew, he says, it just made him respect his father more, because he was so ferociously dedicated to keeping Rudy on the straight path. He loved his son very deeply, and people who knew him during Rudy's childhood described Harold to Barrett as a warm and "huggy" guy.

The unfortunate fact, however, was that Harold's underworld life was not over after he left Sing Sing.

★ ★ ★

Of Helen's five brothers, three grew up to be policemen and one a fireman. But the fifth one, her brother Leo, took a different path. He was the black sheep of the family. In 1948 Leo bought a bar in Brooklyn and embarked upon a very shady career, headquartered in the bar. The bar was called Vincent's. Leo's partner in the bar was a member of the Mafia.

Harold needed steady work to support his family, and his brother-in-law Leo offered it. He went to work for Leo, tending bar and doing various other jobs. He kept a baseball bat behind the bar, and if the patrons became drunk and unruly, he was not afraid to use it. Behind the bar he himself drank glasses of milk to soothe his stomach ulcers.

One of Leo's businesses was being a loan shark. He would lend desperate people money at rates of interest that were so high that the loans were against the law. Since the interest rates were so high, people often fell behind in their payments. That was where Harold came in. He would visit people who owed

Leo money and "convince" them to pay up. It was not a pretty business.

Leo had a son named Lewis. Lewis was a smart boy and did well in school, but Harold watched Lewis hanging around the bar, watching what Leo did. He decided that he wanted to get Rudy away from the bad influence of the bar; it was time to move out of Brooklyn. He wanted a better life for his son. (As it turned out, he was right on target. Lewis grew up to be a gangster, spent time in prison, and was finally killed by the FBI while resisting arrest. He was just thirty-six years old when he died.)

And so, when Rudy was seven, the Giulianis moved to Garden City, Long Island. Adelina sold the house in Brooklyn and used the money for the new place, a neat two-bedroom house on a shady street. Adelina moved in with them, sharing a bedroom with Rudy. The house had a backyard and a basement, where Harold put up a Ping-Pong table and a model train set and hung up a punching bag. It must have been heaven for a boy who had grown up in a second-floor apartment with no place special to play in.

Rudy's new school was also a Catholic school,

with pretty much the same philosophy as his old school: no fooling around. He wore a uniform of blue pants and jacket, blue tie, and white shirt. In school, he learned a mixture of the three R's and Catholic doctrine, with a lot of emphasis on different types of sin and how to avoid them.

One of the nicest parts of Rudy's life was what happened in the summertime. His grandmother Evangelina, his father's mother, had bought a house in Sound Beach, Long Island, and the whole family would gather there on summer weekends. It was a chance for Rudy to get to know his father's side of the family better, because he saw much more of his mother's side. One of the families he always saw at the beach was that of his father's cousin Salvatore Peruggi. Salvatore had three children, two girls named Rita Marie and Regina, and a boy named Richard. Rudy would go down to the beach with his second cousins, and sometimes his father would come along too, usually wearing a business suit.

Harold, meanwhile, was still working at the bar in Brooklyn for Rudy's uncle Leo. But as Rudy grew older Harold seemed to be hating the work more and more. Finally, when Rudy was almost fifteen, Harold had had it with his underworld life. He quit working at Vincent's and instead got a more respectable job, working on the maintenance crew at a high school in Long Island. He helped keep the parking lots and ball fields in good shape, maintained sports equipment, and buffed the floors in the lobby and hallways. A few months later the family bought a house in a town that was closer to Harold's new job.

When it was time for Rudy to go to high school, his parents wanted to make sure that he got the best possible education, while still in a Catholic environment. So they sent him back to Brooklyn, to Bishop Loughlin Memorial High School.

Bishop Loughlin was and still is one of the top Catholic high schools in the city. Being accepted there was hard, and keeping up with the program after getting in was even harder. There was a strict dress code and strict rules of behavior. The school was run by the De La Salle Christian Brothers, and all the classes were taught by brothers in long robes.

Rudy made quite a few new friends at Bishop Loughlin, and two of them were to remain close to him from then on. One of them was Alan Placa, who became a monsignor, a priest with high standing in the Catholic church. Another was Peter Powers, who eventually became Rudy's first deputy mayor. They all spent untold hours at one another's houses, often staying up until the wee hours to talk and argue about politics and religion.

Shortly before this time, Rudy had discovered opera, which had also been the great love of his grandfather Rodolpho. He had gone into a record store near his home on Long Island and picked up a couple of opera records on sale. He took them home and played them, following along with the words that were printed on the album cover. Like his grandfather, he became passionate about opera and contunued buying records.

So the natural thing for Rudy to do in high school was to start an opera club and recruit his buddies for it. Together with all the other members they dragged into the club, they would go to the Metropolitan Opera in Manhattan, or to the Brooklyn Academy of Music. For a dollar and a half, they could buy standing-room tickets to watch the operas.

Rudy had a lot of other extracurricular activities as well. He was elected homeroom president in his freshman year. He played baseball. Later he was on the weightlifting team and the prom committee. Junior year he took his cousin Regina Peruggi to the prom, escorted by both of their fathers. Senior year he was appointed hall monitor, which meant that he had a badge and could issue summonses to student court for rule-breakers. And he also acted as campaign manager for his friend George Schneider, who was running in a hard-fought race for senior class president. He threw himself into the job, working around the clock to get his candidate elected.

Rudy had had his first tastes of law and politics. He liked them both.

He also got a taste of something else: teaching religion. Joining the catechism club, he went out to schools in poor neighborhoods to give children lessons in religion. This struck so deep a chord in him, he briefly considered becoming a priest.

It might be said that Rudy majored in extracurricular activities in high school. In truth, he was not such a great student. By senior year, his average was 84.8—okay, but not outstanding.

But he had begun to settle into the channel that

would soon be carved deeper and deeper into the landscape of his life. At the end of his four years at Bishop Loughlin, in his high school yearbook, he was named "Class Politician."

★CHAPTER THREE★

When Rudy went to college in September of 1961, it was not an altogether new experience. For one thing, his friends Alan Placa and Peter Powers went right along with him. For another, they all enrolled at Manhattan College in the Bronx. This was a Catholic college which was run, like Bishop Loughlin, by the Christian Brothers order. It had strict rules, much like Loughlin's. There were strict regulations about lateness to classes, a dress code, and a prayer before the start of each class. The courses were demanding, as they had been at Loughlin. The students were almost exclusively white, mostly Irish and Italian kids from working-class homes.

Like the majority of his classmates, Rudy was the first one from his family to have the opportunity to go to college. And like them, he also lived at home. This meant a long trek from Long Island, first by railroad and then by subway.

Rudy took his college education seriously,

staying up late to study at home and reading on the train. His grades were much better than they had been in high school. Science and math seemed to be his worst subjects, but in his freshman year he got an A in philosophy.

Another reason his schooling was more urgent now was that his father lost his job in the high school buildings and grounds department. It happened when Rudy was in the second semester of his first year at college. Harold's health was not good, but the reason he lost his job was that he had a sort of mental breakdown and simply stopped showing up for work. In early 1961 Harold had been mistakenly arrested for loitering in the rest room of a Long Island park, though he was doing nothing wrong. He was immediately released without being charged. But the whole experience of being arrested shook him to his core, awakening terrible memories. For a while, he lost the ability to function. Rudy's college education must have been the family's great hope, then more than ever.

Having been bitten in high school by the political bug, Rudy soon got involved in campus politics. Sophomore year he and his friend Peter Powers ran for class office—Rudy for class president, Peter for treasurer.

Rudy and Peter had very different political ideas. Rudy was an ardent supporter of President John F. Kennedy, who was a Democrat. Kennedy was a liberal who believed that government had a positive role to play in the lives of ordinary Americans. Kennedy's brother Robert, whom Rudy also admired very much, became the United States Attorney General in his brother's administration and was passionately committed to wiping out the evil influence of the Mafia once and for all. Peter, on the other hand, was a Republican and was a fervent champion of Senator Barry Goldwater. Goldwater was deeply conservative, an individualist who believed that people were responsible for their own destinies without help from the government.

Rudy and Peter loved having heated political arguments, as they had always done in high school and as Rudy's family had always done at dinner. But it in no way interfered with their friendship. During their campaign for class office, they posted themselves outside classrooms and shook as many hands as they could. They also started their own party, which they called the Eagle Party. Shrewdly they made sure that someone from each branch of the college, such as the engineering and business schools, was represented on their ticket.

Their strategy worked and they won the election. It was Rudy's first victory.

He also had his first real girlfriend in college, a girl from Long Island whom he met while working in a local bank during the summer of his sophomore year. Her name was Kathy Livermore, and she was tall and pretty. They often went on dates to clubs in Manhattan. Rudy was very possessive of her, perhaps because she was so good-looking and he had had so little experience with dating.

Even in college, Rudy was already thinking seriously about a political future. He shared his aspirations with Kathy. Sometimes she would sit with him in his room at home as he practiced delivering speeches.

★ ★ ★

A good route to getting into politics was to become a lawyer first, so that was what Rudy chose as his next step after college. In 1965 he started at New York University's prestigious law school. For the first year he continued to live at home, saving money by commuting into the city. In the second year, however, he moved into a dorm room at school and later into an apartment with the same roommate.

He also got a new girlfriend, who was in reality an old girlfriend. It was his second cousin, Regina Peruggi. They had begun dating again, and their relationship became more and more serious until, in 1968, Rudy asked her to marry him. She said yes.

About a week after they got engaged, Robert Kennedy was shot and killed while campaigning for the presidential nomination. It had been less than five years since his brother John had been assassinated. The nation was devastated. As attorney general, in addition to his fight against organized crime, Bobby Kennedy had been devoted to the cause of civil rights. When a mob threatened violence, he had sent federal marshals in to protect Martin Luther King Jr. and twelve hundred other civil rights marchers in Montgomery, Alabama. Many people, including Rudy, felt he was the nation's great hope, and now he was gone like his brother. It had been only two months since Reverend King had been murdered.

Rudy and Regina went and stood in line with thousands of others to see Bobby's casket at Saint Patrick's Cathedral on Fifth Avenue in Manhattan. Rudy felt that someone irreplaceable had been lost.

★CHAPTER FOUR★

In October of that year Rudy and Regina got married in a church in the Bronx. The wedding was beautiful, and both families and lots of friends attended.

Rudy had started his career that summer. He was now clerking for a federal judge named Lloyd MacMahon. A clerking job is a type of apprenticeship that aspiring young lawyers often try hard to land. Clerks help the judge with various legal tasks, and in turn get an invaluable education in the workings of the judicial system. Having clerked for an influential judge helps a beginning lawyer move up quickly in the legal world.

Judge MacMahon had quite a reputation. He was short-tempered, impatient, and cantankerous and was known to hate lawyers, who frequently returned the favor. He was also a staunch Republican. MacMahon liked young attorneys who had not been born into privilege. Skipping the well-bred Harvard and Yale graduates, he chose as his clerks the ones who had had to fight for their educations, often young Irish and Italian men from working-class families. The judge took Rudy under his wing and became almost a second father to him.

Working for the judge, Rudy toiled for long hours, often getting home long after his new wife had eaten her dinner alone. MacMahon expected his clerks to put a lot into their jobs, and Rudy met his expectations.

In 1970 Rudy Giuliani's hard work bore fruit. He became an assistant United States district attorney for the Southern District of New York. Judge MacMahon had recommended him for the job. Rudy, wearing a big mustache of a style that was very popular at the time, stood between his father and his wife as he was sworn in.

Now he was really on his way. Being in the U.S. attorney's office meant catching criminals, prosecuting them, and putting them away. It meant he could have a place to continue the effort Bobby Kennedy had begun to break the power of organized crime. It was also a good place to begin a path to a life in politics.

Rudy won the first case he ever argued in front

of a jury. Then he kept winning and winning. By his count, in the five years he worked in the U.S. attorney's office, he tried thirty-two cases and lost only two. After one of these two losses, he decided that the jury hadn't liked his mustache, so he shaved it off.

His work at the U.S. attorney's office also led to an experience that gave Rudy his first taste of fame, at least indirectly. In 1981 a movie called *Prince of the City* came out. It was all about crime-busting prosecutors at the New York district attorney's office, and one of the main characters was a tough but good-natured prosecutor named Mario Vincente. He was modeled on Rudy Giuliani.

One of the most important experiences he had as an assistant D.A. was while he was working on the case of a man named William Phillips.

A couple of years before Rudy started in the D.A.'s office, New Yorkers had been shocked to discover that their police department was riddled with corruption and bribery. While most cops were honorable, some were not. Some cops took money from drug dealers, accepted bribes from organized crime, or stole drugs from evidence rooms. Once the rocks began to be turned over, the nasty discoveries went on and on. The disease had to be rooted out and killed, and it was a big, unpleasant job. A special commission was formed to get some results.

William Phillips was a "dirty cop," one who had been corrupt for his whole career. Once he was found out, he made a deal with the prosecutors. He went undercover and informed on his fellow police officers to avoid being prosecuted himself.

Phillips told Rudy shocking things. He said that he had gone into the police force to reap the rewards of corruption. His father had been a policeman before him and had joined the Force for the same reason. Naturally, Phillips explained to Rudy, once you had taken money from a mobster, you had to look the other way if you saw a little bit of murder. It wouldn't do to arrest the mobster and have him tell on you.

These revelations shook Rudy to the core. He had never imagined that such cynical and dirty things could be going on in his beloved city. It is likely that his own uncle Leo, his cousin Lewis, and perhaps even his father had been involved in similar doings, but Rudy had been protected from these realities for his whole life. Rudy found that his whole view of the human race was undergoing a change. "I had this youthful conviction that all human beings were basically good," he said later. "If you just turned on the right switch, goodness and rationality would flow forth. I came to realize that rationality does not necessarily rule and that some people were simply evil. There was very little you could do to change them, and if you entertained the romantic notion that they could be changed, you would wind up endangering innocent people."

It is unlikely that what happened on September 11 changed Rudy Giuliani's view of human nature.

Rudy's next job was in Washington, D.C. In 1975 Lloyd MacMahon had recommended him again, this time for a job in the Justice Department under President Gerald Ford. There he got a close-up view of how government worked. He developed a sharp disrespect for members of Congress, and he showed it. His boss at the Justice Department decided he had better steer Rudy away from dealing with them. Rudy worked on "white-collar crime"—crimes that did not involve violence, but rather were committed, for example, by accountants stealing from their companies, or businesses stealing from their customers or each other. They were not easy crimes to prose-cute, because they were so complicated, but Rudy went at it with great energy. While he was in Washington, the Giulianis led an active social life, and Rudy made a number of powerful friends in the government. Regina, however, was not of the same outgoing nature as Rudy and did not seem to like all the parties very much.

★ ★ ★

Rudy's job in Washington lasted for only a year and a half until Jimmy Carter, a Democrat, defeated Gerald Ford in the next election. That meant more Democrats would be appointed to the Justice Department, and the Republicans would be out. It was time to pack up and go back to New York. Rudy, along with a number of the lawyers he worked with in the Justice Department, got jobs at a prestigious law firm in New York called Patterson, Belknap and Webb. Now he was on the opposite side from where he had been as a prosecutor. He was defending people accused of crimes instead of trying to put them behind bars.

Rudy and his wife had been steadily growing apart. They lived under the same roof, but lived basically separate lives. Finally in 1980 they separated.

And then that same year Carter was defeated in his reelection bid, and a Republican, Ronald Reagan, was once again in the White House. Back to Washington Rudy went, but now he was in a much higher-level position. On May 15, 1981, he was sworn in as associate attorney general of the United States. That made him the number three man in the Justice Department. He was the youngest person ever to be named to the job.

Rudy's personal victory was tinged with sadness, however. Less than a month before he was sworn in, his father had died of cancer in New York. Rudy had been flying back and forth from Washington to New York as his father had gotten sicker and sicker. When Harold died, Rudy felt the loss deeply. "My father gave me a great gift," he said later. "He gave me an internal sense of how to find a positive way to deal with whatever life has in store for you. But I lost a great source of strength when he died."

While Rudy was serving that term in Washington, he was involved in a chapter of history that most people agree did not bring out the best part of him. If Rudy Giuliani has two sides, one tough and one tender, this was an example of the tough-Rudy side. It involved immigrants from the island country of Haiti.

Haiti had been through decades of horror. For many years, a dictator named François Duvalier, nicknamed "Papa Doc," had been in control of Haiti. He had ruled with an iron hand, and anyone who dared oppose him was imprisoned, tortured, or killed. When he died in 1971, his eighteen-year-old son Jean-Claude had taken over. Jean-Claude simply continued his father's reign of terror, and was contemptuously dubbed "Baby Doc" by the people of Haiti. He and his father were responsible for the deaths of at least sixty thousand people and stole much of the aid money that was given to Haiti by foreign countries, leaving the people impoverished.

Because life was so terrible in Haiti, thousands of people tried to escape. Many of them got into rickety boats and headed toward the United States. The United States did not want them, and it was President Reagan's aim to stop them from coming and send them home if they reached American shores. One of Rudy Giuliani's main jobs was to carry out this policy.

Thousands of people were also escaping from

Cuba in boats, but theirs was a different story. Because the United States was opposed to the Communist government of Cuba, the refugees were welcomed here. The U.S., however, was friendly to the government of Duvalier, and so Haitian refugees found no welcome.

Rudy Giuliani saw to it that U.S. Coast Guard ships were sent into the waters between Haiti and the U.S. to stop the boatfuls of Haitians and turn them back. This was despite a great deal of evidence that many who had tried to escape were caught and killed when they returned to Haiti. He also ended a longstanding policy of allowing the Haitian refugees who made it here to be taken care of by church groups and families, and instead, began putting them into detention camps. There they were so miserable and frightened that scores of them attempted suicide.

At one point a Coast Guard ship stopped a boat carrying 161 fleeing Haitians. The ship had also picked up two Cuban refugees whose boat had sunk. The Coast Guard sent the Haitians back to Haiti, but let the Cubans enter the U.S.

Rudy even traveled to Haiti, where he was entertained by Baby Doc and assured that anyone who was sent back to Haiti would not be harmed. Rudy chose to believe him, despite all the evidence to the contrary.

Eventually the issue of the detention camps went to court, and the judge ruled that the camps were illegal and the Haitians had to be let go. Rudy, with the same zeal he had used to prosecute criminals, kept on fighting, bringing the case to higher and higher courts. They all ruled against him. The whole issue was beginning to make the government look bad, especially since the Haitians were all black, which led to accusations of racial discrimination. But Rudy believed his policy was right and the courts were wrong. Besides, the plan of sending escaping Haitians back to Haiti and putting the rest into detention camps was having the effect he and President Reagan wanted. For the most part, the Haitians stopped trying to come to the U.S.

By 1983 all the Haitians had been released from the detention camps. But by then, Rudy was on his way back home to New York.

★Chapter Five★

On June 3, 1983, Rudy Giuliani went back to the same office in which he'd gotten his start, the U.S. attorney's office for the Southern District in New York. Only this time, he *was* the U.S. attorney—the top man. His mother had argued against the move, believing that it was a step down to go from being Number Three in the Justice Department in Washington back to a local office in New York. But Rudy decided to do it, because he felt he could have more of an impact as the biggest fish in a smaller pond. In New York he had over a hundred attorneys working under him, and he was, once again, the youngest person ever to have held the job.

A new job was not all he had when he returned to New York. He also had a new woman in his life. She was a pretty television reporter named Donna Hanover. Rudy had met her while he had been working in the Justice Department. Dealing with the issue of the Haitians had frequently taken him to

Miami, where Donna was working at a television station. They began seeing each other, and she had finally moved to Washington to be with him, and they were married in 1983. Rudy and Regina, meanwhile, had quietly divorced the year before.

As U.S. attorney, Rudy had a lot of plans. He wanted to make big changes and do big things. He began increasing his staff of attorneys and fighting crime, big-time.

His first target was his longtime enemy, organized crime. Building upon work that had begun before his return to New York, Rudy began putting together evidence that would put a lot of Mafia bosses away for a long time. He realized that his best chance of prosecuting them was to use the Racketeer Influenced and Corrupt Organizations (RICO) laws. These laws were often used to build cases against large businesses that were racketeering, or operating in unfair and illegal ways. Carefully, over a long period, he put together large, complicated charts that showed the organization of the five large Mafia families in New York. The heads of these families were known as a group as "the Commission." Rudy argued that the Commission was run just like a large business, and could be prosecuted in the same way. The Commission controlled almost all the construction, garbage hauling, and various other businesses in the city. One Mafioso bragged that not a yard of concrete was poured in the city without the mob's say-so.

On the night of February 25, 1985, Rudy saw all his dogged and careful work bear fruit in a spectacular way. That night, fifty mob bosses, with names like "Fat Tony" Salerno, Carmine "The Snake" Persico, and Tony "Ducks" Corallo, were arrested in a huge sweep and marched downtown to the courthouse to be booked. Waiting for this show was a horde of television and newspaper cameras. Rudy stood on the steps of the courthouse and spoke to the media about how justice was being done at long last. It was a glorious moment for the good guys.

Rudy didn't stop there, either. He went after dishonest Wall Street traders and crooked politicians, often making sure that they were photographed in handcuffs as they were led away.

Rudy Giuliani was making a name for himself as a tough, crime-busting prosecutor. Everyone in the city knew who he was, though they probably could not have named his predecessor. People around New

York began to feel that it was only a matter of time until he moved up to the next level. He considered running for U.S. Senate, but finally decided not to.

In May of 1989, however, Rudy announced that he was running for mayor. He wrote his announcement speech himself, speaking eloquently about the shame of homelessness and the taint of corruption in New York. "As a candidate for mayor and as mayor," he said, "I am seeking support on one basis and one basis alone—that you agree with me that honest, decent, and effective government must be restored. If you offer support or money expecting any special deals," he went on, "forget about it, save your money. Let me repeat one more time—no deals for jobs, no deals for contributors." He went on to talk about his career in law enforcement. "As mayor," he said, "I will instill a sense of fear in those who commit serious crimes."

The speech ended with a soaring, heartfelt declaration: "This is the city of my roots," Rudy said. "It is in my heart and it is in my soul. My grandparents and my father are buried in the soil of this city. All of my past draws me to take on this challenge, to restore the city of my grandparents and parents, of my relatives and my friends, and to offer New Yorkers hope for the future once again."

When the dust cleared after the primaries, and all the other mayoral hopefuls had been winnowed out, the race boiled down to Rudy, a Republican, against David Dinkins, a courtly, grandfatherly black Democrat. The campaign had become nastier, and a couple of unpleasant racial incidents, not handled well by Rudy's advisers, had added an ugly cast to things.

New York is traditionally a tough town for a Republican to win; it usually elects Democrats. On election day the Democrat won by only 44,000 votes, a tiny margin. David Dinkins became New York's first African-American mayor.

By this time Rudy and Donna had two children: Andrew, born in 1986, and Caroline, in 1989. Donna had gotten a job reporting the news at WPIX, a television station in New York.

After the election, Rudy went back into private legal practice, but what interested him most was planning for his next move: another run for mayor in four years. He was convinced he could win next time.

★ ★ ★

By 1993 New York City had undergone a serious and unhappy change. David Dinkins was a well-intentioned and gentlemanly mayor, but he had lost hold of the quality of life in the city. Citizens could not walk a block, it seemed, or get onto a subway car, or stop their cars at a traffic light, without being accosted by a homeless person asking for money. Cars parked on the street displayed hopeful little homemade NO RADIO signs to discourage thieves from breaking in. The city's finances had taken a nosedive, and 59 percent of the residents said in a poll that they would move out of the city if they could. *Time* magazine published a story titled "The Rotting of the Big Apple." New York was widely believed to be ungovernable, and the city's morale was in the basement.

It was a perfect opportunity for a "tough cop" like Rudy Giuliani to step in and take hold of things. He campaigned on a promise to clean up the small quality-of-life crimes, like panhandlers menacing passersby to get money, or men with squeegees who intimidated people into letting them clean their windshields for a quarter. His reasoning was that when small crimes like that went unpunished, the whole tone of civilized society began to fall apart. It was called the "broken window" theory—that if a vandal threw a rock at a window of a building, and nobody fixed it, pretty soon all the windows would be broken, and the neighborhood would be given over to the vandals.

Dinkins dismissed this idea, saying that "real" crime like murder or robbery was the only thing the police needed to be concerned with. But Rudy had hit a nerve with the weary population of the city. Some people began to imagine life without these daily encounters that exhausted them. They began to want the life that Rudy was promising them.

There were many, however, who feared that Giuliani's policies would amount to a war against people who were simply guilty of being poor. The campaign wore on, and the numbers were so close that nobody could predict the outcome of the election. Even during the course of election day, reports of who was winning kept changing.

Finally after midnight, the winner was announced. Rudy Giuliani had been elected mayor by

45,000 votes, nearly the same narrow margin by which he had lost in 1989.

On a cold Sunday morning, January 2, 1994, Rudy was sworn in as the 107th mayor of New York. On the stand in City Hall Park with him were his wife, his children, and his mother, Helen. He looked strikingly similar to his mother—same mouth that went down at the corners, same straight nose, same high forehead. His son, Andrew, was clearly as wiggly a child as his father had once been, mugging for the cameras and repeating his father's lines. Rudy didn't mind a bit. He was having a great day.

"The era of fear has had a long enough reign," he told the crowd. "The period of doubt has run its course. As of this moment, the expressions of cynicism—New York is not governable, New York is not manageable, New York is not worth it—all of these I declare politically incorrect."

Now New York was about to get to know the real Rudy.

He started keeping his promises immediately, bringing in a police commissioner with a reputation for getting things done. His name was William Bratton, and he came from Boston. Bratton shared

Rudy's belief in the "broken window" theory of law enforcement. "We will fight for every house in the city," he announced when he first spoke to the New York press. "We will fight for every street. We will fight for every borough. And we will win." He sounded like a Wild West good-guy cowboy in a white hat, riding in to clean up the town. The newspapers loved it.

On Bratton's very first day on the job, January 9, he got his first test before he was even out of the airport. Someone called in a burglary-in-progress at a mosque in Harlem, the central location for the Nation of Islam, a black Muslim group. When the police got there, however, they did not know that they were in a house of worship, and a scuffle ensued between the cops and Muslim security guards, who were outraged at the storming of a mosque. (Later it turned out the robbery call had not even been real; it had been a hoax.) The cops got thrown down the stairs, and the security guards took a gun and a radio from one of them. It turned into a near-riot, and because Bratton had not arrived in town yet, Rudy was giving the orders. He wanted arrests. He wanted to start showing that the police were not going to be pushed around anymore. Order was going to be maintained. The situation teetered very close to becoming a riot, but finally cooled off.

Rudy was not interested in meeting with the city's black leaders to discuss the problem. They were miffed, he was miffed. Eventually the situation blew over, but the new administration had started with a jolt. Rudy, it was clear, was not going to make nice if he did not believe it was in the best interest of the city. People in all neighborhoods, rich and poor, were going to be safer. The police were going to be respected, and order was going to prevail. Sometimes Rudy liked to quote what his father had said to him when he was young: "It's better to be respected than to be loved. Eventually, you will love me."

One important part of the new war on crime was a huge computer system that the administration put into place. With it, the police could track crime in every neighborhood, on every block, just as William Bratton had said. If they found that crime had increased in a small pocket of the city, more police officers could be sent there to find out what was going on and stop it.

With this new approach, the crime rate began to go down at a breathtaking rate. Within three months of Rudy's inauguration, crime was down by double digits. But more safety for all of New York's citizens did come at a price, one which some people felt was high. Because of the new emphasis on small quality-of-life crimes, arrests for minor offenses skyrocketed. Squeegee men were put on notice that they would no longer be able to wash windshields for quarters, and they were cleared off the streets. Young people who jumped the turnstiles to beat the subway fares were arrested. Anybody who was caught spraying graffiti on a wall or bothering someone was nabbed and hauled into the police station.

Leaders of the minority communities had mixed feelings. On one hand, people were beginning to feel safer on the streets. This was especially true in poor neighborhoods, where ordinary people were most often preyed upon by criminals. But on the other hand, the broad police net was pulling in many more people from these same communities. Thousands of young minority men were going to jail.

Whatever reservations there might have been,

though, the mood of the city was definitely changing. People were feeling hopeful again. Tourists were coming back, having stayed away from the dark, scary metropolis for years. Times Square, which had been a seedy, tawdry, embarrassing area, suddenly blossomed into a glittery, neon-bright wonderland. English-style double-decker buses ferried out-of-towners around Manhattan as they snapped photos of the hustle and bustle. Money began flowing into the city again. The streets were cleaner. The parks were safer and prettier.

And New York began getting used to the personal style of their new mayor. "He gave the city the clear sense that somebody was in charge," said Chris McNickle, who had written a book about New York politics. "At the same time, when a mayor has that strong a personality, he often leaves people with the impression that there's no room for opposition or alternate views."

There was, for example, the education battle. A few months after he took office, the new mayor got into a major battle with Chancellor of Education Ramon Cortines. Cortines was a soft-spoken, thoughtful man, and was well liked. Coming from

California, he had turned down an important job in Washington because he wanted to try to better New York's public schools, which were known to be in terrible shape.

Rudy felt that the mayor should have more power over the city's educational system. He also felt that there were too many useless employees in the system. He announced that 2,500 workers would need to be eliminated from the system. Cortines refused. Rudy badgered him. Cortines said he would quit. The governor of New York State, Mario Cuomo, finally helped them work out a compromise, but the battles continued. Rudy pushed, Cortines pushed back. The public began to feel that Rudy was bullying the chancellor, and it showed in the polls. But Rudy, true to form, did not care about the polls. He cared about fixing the schools, and he felt that only his answer was the right one. He told Cortines to stop whining. Finally in 1995, Cortines quit.

New Yorkers were getting to know the mayor who cared more about being respected than liked. In a poll taken some time after the Cortines affair, over half of the public said they didn't think Rudy had a likeable personality. But over 60 percent of them still felt he was doing a good job. So Rudy was right.

Then there were the police problems. On August 9, 1997, a Haitian immigrant named Abner Louima, who lived in Brooklyn, was picked up by the police, taken to the police station, and tortured in a bathroom there. He had done nothing wrong, but he was almost killed. He spent weeks in the hospital.

Then, on February 4, 1999, police officers, while searching for a man who had committed several rapes, cornered a man in the lobby of a Harlem building. Thinking he had a gun, they shot him forty-four times. It was a case of mistaken identity. The man's name was Amadou Diallo, and he was a street vendor who had recently come to New York from Africa in search of a better life. Instead, he was killed. Rudy Giuliani made no apologies, even when Diallo's parents arrived from Africa to protest.

And finally, there was the case of Patrick Dorismond, an unarmed security guard, also Haitian, who was shot by undercover narcotics detectives on his night off. There was no good reason for the shooting.

All three men were black. Taken together, these

incidents served to convince the public that Rudy Giuliani, in the name of lowering the crime rate, had allowed the police to run amok. Many felt there was no longer any care for defenseless people of color who were just minding their own business and trying to live their lives. Rudy, true to form, did not do a good job of reassuring those who were upset. In fact, in the case of Patrick Dorismond, he released the record of a years-old minor crime, to show that the man was "no altar boy." This only served to make people more incensed.

Nobody went around accusing Rudy Giuliani of being sensitive.

Still, he had won reelection in 1997 with no difficulty. It did not, however, escape anyone's notice that his wife Donna did not appear with him on election night. People who knew what was going on in Gracie Mansion, the mayor's home, knew that their marriage was no longer a happy one.

Then in September of 1999, there was Rudy's battle with the Brooklyn Museum. It started when a reporter called Rudy to ask what he thought about the controversial new show, called "Sensation," that was about to open at the Brooklyn Museum. At the time, Rudy was busy with other things. Hurricane Floyd, which had devastated the South, was possibly on its way up to the city. Rudy and his advisers were hunkered down at the recently built thirteen-million-dollar Emergency Operations Center on the twenty-third floor at Seven World Trade Center, planning for school closings and emergency shelter. (Rudy had been ridiculed for spending so much money on the command center, which was called "Rudy's bunker." He was, of course, later proved right about the need for it. Its only problem turned out to be the location.)

Rudy knew little about the museum exhibit, and besides, he was busy. He brushed the question off. But the storm came and went, and questions about the art show kept coming, until Rudy finally paid attention. He had someone bring him a catalog to look at. What he saw outraged him and his advisers. The show was meant to be shocking, and it had the desired effect. It included, for example, a dead cow cut into twelve slices and preserved in formaldehyde in separate glass cases. There was also a picture of an African Virgin Mary, adorned with elephant dung. There were lots of other pieces that evoked extreme reactions. Rudy called it "sick stuff."

Rudy's reaction was swift. He announced that the city would cut off the seven million dollars that it contributed each year to the museum's upkeep. He was also considering throwing the museum out of its building, owned by the city. And he created a special "decency commission" to study art in city-funded institutions.

None of this was popular in a sophisticated, art-loving city like New York. Its residents were behind the museum and against Rudy, by a margin of two to one. In fact, the publicity was very good for the museum. When the exhibit opened, the lines went around the block. Thirteen thousand people attended on the first day. Ultimately, Rudy's threats against the museum were blocked in court, and none of them were carried out. But Rudy did not care; for him, the fight was a matter of principle. He went on the television news programs to denounce the show.

It was almost time for Rudy's maximum two terms to end. He was thinking about where to set his sights next. He decided to run for United States

Senate, against former First Lady Hillary Clinton. It promised to be a close, no-holds-barred fight.

And then, in the spring of 2000, everything fell apart in a spectacular way.

On April 27, Rudy announced to the city that he had prostate cancer. Prostate cancer affects a gland that only males have, and was the same kind of cancer that had killed Rudy's father. The city was stunned.

But that was only the beginning of the roller-coaster ride. Just a week later, on May 3, the *New York Post* published a photo of Rudy with a woman who was not his wife. Rudy told New Yorkers that she was "a very good friend." Rumors began flying around the city that Rudy and the woman, Judith Nathan, had been in a relationship for quite a while.

Three days later Donna pledged her support of her husband, with whom she had not been seen in public in years. "This man and this marriage have been very precious to me," she said.

Then, another bombshell: Rudy told reporters outside a restaurant that his marriage to Donna was essentially over, that they led separate lives, and that they would soon be formalizing a legal separation.

The only problem was, he had not told Donna about this decision. Now she was on the warpath, very publicly. And Donna Hanover was no shrinking violet.

Rudy's life had suddenly exploded. His personal life was plastered all over the newspapers. He had to choose a treatment for his cancer, and he was still trying to decide whether to keep running for Senate. His war with Donna turned horribly messy, with lawyers trading nasty charges in the newspapers. He was seen openly with his new flame, and Donna threatened to throw him out of Gracie Mansion. And of course he was still the mayor of New York.

The city held its breath, waiting for Rudy to say something.

Finally on May 19, he did. He called a press conference, and hundreds of reporters and photographers and cameramen waited for him to appear. When at last he strode into the room, he looked pale and gaunt and suddenly much older.

The audience gave him a standing ovation, this man who had been through so much, so publicly, in the last few weeks. And when he began to talk, a totally new Rudy seemed to be speaking.

"I'm a very fortunate man," he said. "God has given me a lot, and whatever obstacles that are placed in your way, I think the way to deal with it is to try to figure out how to make it make you a better person." It could almost have been his father, Harold, speaking at that moment. "The reason I'm such a fortunate man is that I have people that love me and I love them, and they care for me and I care for them. And that's the greatest support that you can have in life."

New York's collective jaw dropped. This was a Rudy they had never, ever heard.

He went on to talk about how "something beautiful happens" when one is confronted with big problems. "It makes you figure out what you're all about and what's really important to you," he said. He said that he had always thought that politics had been the most important thing in his life, but that he had decided it wasn't. He was going to put his health first. He was dropping out of the Senate race. "I thank God it gives me, really, another eighteen months to be the mayor of New York City," he said. He went on to promise the city's minorities that he was going to try very hard to make them feel the changes that he was undergoing. Rudy said he was going to do better.

After it was over, one city councilman compared Rudy to Ebenezer Scrooge in Charles Dickens's *A Christmas Carol*, after he'd been visited by the Ghost of Christmas Future.

★CHAPTER SIX★

By August of 2001 Rudy was coasting toward the finish line. The *New York Times* conducted a poll of city dwellers, and found that they held a sunnier view of their city and its future than they had in over twenty-five years. In 2001 violent crime made its biggest drop in five years. Crime in general was down more than 12 percent over the year before, and the number of murders in the city fell from 671 to 640. (This is in contrast to the high point of New York City mayhem: 1,927 murders in 1993.) Certainly, the booming economy had played a big part in the revival of the city. But most people gave Rudy a lot of the credit as well, and while crime was beginning to climb in other cities as the economy worsened, New York's crime rate stayed down.

Of course, this was not a fairy tale, and Rudy did not stop being Rudy. In March he went to a meeting of educators at the Board of Education to talk about his ideas, which were so unpopular that he was roundly booed. He was also still at war with Donna, and New York was getting a little tired of it. Their squabbles, lawsuits, and countersuits had filled the papers for months. In May he had cut her office staff, along with her security guards, to diminish her power. Finally he moved out of Gracie Mansion and into the apartment of friends. Even though most New Yorkers felt great about the city, Rudy's popularity hovered around 50 percent in the polls, as it had for a couple of years. By midsummer a heated race was on for the mayoralty. Rudy told the press he was looking forward to the day when he could simply live his life, without being followed and badgered by reporters. He was ready for the next chapter of his life.

★ ★ ★

Beautiful days are precious in New York. The weather in the city usually careens from sweltering heat to wind-whipped cold. But the morning of September 11 was gorgeous—a clear, blue sky, the perfect temperature.

At eight o'clock in the morning, Rudy was having a breakfast meeting with Denny Young, one of his aides, and a friend who was running for governor of

U.S. Attorney Giuliani baby-sitting son at home, January 1987

U.S. Attorney Giuliani speaking at a press conference, July 1987

**Federal Prosecutor Rudolph Giuliani riding the subway,
New York City, 1989**

Bill Clinton and Rudolph Giuliani, October 1994

Giuliani family attends Pope John Paul II's visit to Central Park, New York, October 1995

Mayor Giuliani, 1997

Mayor Giuliani and retired General Colin Powell join Janet Jackson to announce her benefit concert tour, March 1998

George Pataki and Mayor Giuliani shake hands during a joint session of congress on Capitol Hill, September 2001. First Lady Laura Bush and British Prime Minister Tony Blair are among those applauding them.

**Mayor Giuliani embraces mayoral candidate
Mike Bloomberg at a press conference, New York, October 2001**

**The U.S. flag flies at
half-staff in front of
the site of the World
Trade Center attack,
November 2001**

**U.S. Secretary of Defense
Donald Rumsfeld's first
tour of Ground Zero,
November 14, 2001**

**President George W. Bush speaks with Mayor Giuliani during a
Veterans Day breakfast, November, 2001**

From left: Governor George Pataki, President George W. Bush, Mayor Giuliani, and New York Police Commissioner Bernard Kerik all bow in prayer during a Veterans Day breakfast, New York, November 2001

Indian Prime Minister Atal Bihari Vajpayee and Mayor Giuliani tour Ground Zero, November 14, 2001

The Emir of Qatar Sheik Hamad bin Khalifa al-Thani with Mayor Giuliani after touring Ground Zero

Mayor Giuliani lights the Olympic flame in New York, December 2001

California. They had met at the elegant Peninsula Hotel in midtown Manhattan.

Toward the end of breakfast, at about eight forty-five, Denny Young's cell phone rang. It was Joe Lhota, the deputy mayor. The mayor needed to get downtown right away. A plane had hit the north tower of the World Trade Center, about three miles to the south of where they were.

Rudy, like just about everybody else in New York, had trouble getting his mind to accept this news. "How could this happen?" he later told *Time* magazine he'd thought. "Airplanes don't hit the World Trade Center."

They sped downtown in the mayor's waiting sports-utility vehicle to meet other officials at the scene. Many, like Lhota, had been close by, at City Hall, when it happened. On the way downtown, the Mayor's car passed a hospital in Greenwich Village, about forty blocks from the World Trade Center. There were doctors and nurses milling around in operating gowns, waiting with stretchers for the injured. This was when the terrible reality began to hit.

Because the transmitters were at the top of the World Trade Center, all the cell phones in the area had stopped working. This made communication much more difficult—and communication was key.

The mayor raced to the emergency command center at Seven World Trade Center. But as they arrived, the building, which was right next to Towers One and Two, was in the process of being evacuated. A few hours later, it would collapse like the towers.

Now all bets were off. The secure place that was supposed to serve as a nerve center in case of any catastrophe was unusable. And this catastrophe was almost beyond the power of imagination. How would the mayor act as a leader if he had no place to lead from? The command center was filled with computers, maps, survival gear, and communications equipment. And now there was nothing, not even cell phones.

Outside the building Rudy searched for key people from the police and fire departments, and for his deputies. Then the group started walking, looking for a place to work from, looking for phones that worked on old-fashioned wires.

At this point only the North Tower had been hit. Nobody knew if it had been some colossal accident—a plane gone horribly astray—or if it was no accident at all. And certainly, nobody was expecting another hit.

Rudy's mind was working a mile a minute. Manhattan island would have to be sealed off immediately. No one must be able to get in or out. Had the bridges and tunnels been closed? If this was terrorism, were the terrorists planning to attack those as well?

And then there was the air space above New York. Were planes still flying over the city? Had the air lanes been closed off? Who would give the order to do this? Rudy and his police commissioner, Bernard Kerik, talked about what to do. They needed to call the White House. Cut off from all their emergency information, they did not even know who would give the order to shut down air traffic. Certainly it would not be the police commissioner of New York.

The group began walking north, looking for a place to set up some sort of headquarters.

Downtown Manhattan is a place of tall, dark canyons and narrow streets. From the ground, it is usual not to see the tops of buildings that are just a block away, because of the precipitous angles. And so, when the mayor and his group turned south onto West Street, a broad avenue that runs along the western edge of the island, he got his first real view of what was going on. "No matter how it was described," he told *Time*, "it's much worse. The top of the building is totally in flames. I look up, and for some reason, my eye catches the top of the World Trade Center, and I see a man jump—it must have been one hundred stories up."

It was then, said the police commissioner, that Rudy really "kicked into overdrive." It seemed as if all of the mayor's zealous attention to detail, all of his legendary ability to focus like a laser beam, had crystallized in this moment of history.

The first place they reached, three blocks away, was the Fire Department's temporary command post. There, Fire Chief Peter Ganci told the mayor that the important thing was to tell people to remain calm, that the firefighters were on their way up. "I think we can save everybody below the fire," he told the mayor, which Rudy understood immediately to mean that everyone above the fire was lost. At least, he thought, the firefighters would be safe. They would never be able to work their way up above the fire, where they would be in danger.

He took Peter Ganci's hand and shook it. Then they exchanged a quick hug. "Good luck," Rudy said. "God bless you." He did the same with First Deputy Commissioner Bill Feehan, and Battalion Chief Ray Downey, for whom he had recently given a dinner at Gracie Mansion. He waved to them, never imagining that this would be their last good-bye.

There was one fire official he wanted to keep with him, though: Thomas Von Essen, the fire commissioner. He wanted both the police and fire commissioners available to make decisions together, as they came up. Von Essen wanted to stay at the Trade Center, but Rudy called for him, and of course he had to go. He is probably alive today, he speculates, because of this decision.

By this time, the second plane was slicing through the air toward the South Tower. When it crashed into the building, there was no doubt anymore: this was no accident. This was terrorism.

The mayor's group made their way into a nearby office building at Seventy-five Barclay Street. They commandeered a group of evacuated cubicles on the ground floor and began working the phones. One of the mayor's aides got through to an official at the White House, who told Rudy that another hijacked plane had plowed into the Pentagon and that fighter planes had been sent to protect the city. He also said that the vice president was going to try to call back, but that right then they were evacuating the White House.

Rudy hung up the phone. "My God," he said, "I never thought I'd have that conversation. They're evacuating the White House."

Vice President Dick Cheney did try to get through to the mayor in a few minutes, but was unable to hold on to a connection. But while Rudy was trying to get the phone to work, someone burst in and yelled, "Hit the deck!"

There was an enormous rumble, like a thousand freight trains going by. It felt as if an earthquake had hit. All the outside windows shattered, and the room instantly filled with black smoke, ash, dust, and debris. Nobody knew what had happened.

Up to this point, it was totally unthinkable that the World Trade Center could collapse. The buildings were hugely strong because of the networks of steel sheathing that traveled up their sides. When the towers had been built, beginning in 1966, the architects had been careful to plan for the utmost strength. The biggest worry that people had had at that time was the wind: Would structures that tall be able to handle the whistling winds that would buffet them at that altitude? (In high winds, the towers could actually be felt swaying; they were designed to do this.) Because the buildings were so tall, a great deal of thought had also been spent making the buildings able to withstand an accidental collision from an airplane. But back then, there were no jets carrying tons of flammable jet fuel. And nobody, absolutely nobody, was thinking about huge acts of terrorism on American soil.

In the building on Barclay Street, unable to see what was going on outside, Rudy was still not thinking in terms of a building collapse. His conjecture was that the radio tower, an enormous 360-foot spike on top of Tower One, had fallen down.

The officials held a hasty conference and made the decision to evacuate the building. They made their way to the basement and tried several exits, but every one was locked. When they came back upstairs, everything was worse outside. The air was filled with smoke and dust and flying papers. They were trapped.

Then two security guards who worked in the building turned up, telling the mayor and his staff that there was one exit downstairs which led to the next building over. They might be able to get out from that building. The men led the group downstairs and through a maze of tunnels. "I'm thinking, I hope these doors aren't locked," Rudy told *Time*. "And for the first time, very slightly, the thought enters my mind: We could get trapped here."

But the security guards knew what they were talking about. They were not trapped. The door pushed open, and they found themselves in the lobby of the adjoining building, One Hundred Church Street. The air outside was opaque; they could see no one.

The revolving door turned, and in walked a man who was completely coated in white dust. His eyes were bleeding. Somehow, Police Commissioner Kerik recognized him as one of his deputy commissioners, a man whom he had known for many years. His name was Tibor Kerekes. The mayor knew him well also, because he was on the mayor's security team. A fearless man with a black belt in karate, he was utterly devastated. He was shaking. "It's terrible out there," he said. "Terrible."

The worst had indeed happened: the South Tower, the second one to be hit, had been the first to fall.

Kerekes told the mayor that when the building had begun to collapse, he had dashed into a nearby entryway, which had protected him. If he had not found that small bit of shelter, he would have been crushed.

A hurried conference was held among the mayor's group. Some people wanted to stay put until things cleared up. But Rudy would not hear of it. The people of his city needed to hear from him. He wanted to begin communicating with them, and he wanted to set up the city's government some-where. And, though he did not say it, he felt that if he was going to die, he wanted to be outside and not trapped in a building.

Out they went into the choking air. When they emerged on the corner of West Broadway and Church Street, they found, by chance, a small group of local reporters who knew the mayor well. "We're taking you with us," said Rudy. As they all began moving up West Broadway, he proceeded to hold a walking press conference, telling the reporters that people needed to stay calm and walk straight north, as they themselves were doing. As they walked the mayor was trying to find a phone he could use to speak to the White House, and he was also herding everyone they passed on the street northward.

Up above, they heard the roar of a plane in the sky. Everyone on the ground began to panic: More planes! What were they going to bomb next? But then somebody yelled, "It's ours!" To the enormous relief of the crowds below, a U.S. Navy fighter jet zoomed into view overhead.

But now there was a second gigantic rumbling: the North Tower, and they were out in the open. A huge cloud of dust and smoke and pulverized concrete came hurtling down the street behind them, and the whole group began running for their lives.

They ran into the Tribeca Grand, which had been a busy luxury hotel just a couple of hours before. Perhaps they could set up a headquarters there. But looking up, they saw that the huge lobby was completely made of glass. It was too vulnerable. They would have to move on.

Thomas Von Essen, the fire commissioner, remembered that there was a firehouse nearby, Engine Company Twenty-four. They made for it, but discovered when they reached it that it was locked. The whole fire company had gone to the Twin Towers.

Someone jimmied the door open, and they were in. The mayor immediately held his first real press conference. Then they began working the phones again, calling all the people with whom they had not been in touch. Rudy spoke to George Pataki, the governor of New York, who had of course been frantically trying to reach him. Then he spoke to Donna and made sure she and the children were all right, and after that he called Judith Nathan.

It was at the firehouse that they learned that Bill Feehan and Pete Ganci, to whom Rudy had said good-bye perhaps an hour before, were dead. Ray Downey was gone, as was Father Mychal Judge, the Fire Department's chaplain. Senior officers with long histories in the Fire Department, they represented a huge loss. Nobody knew how many other firefighters, police officers, and other rescue workers were also gone.

They stayed there for about three quarters of an hour, but they would have to move again. They needed more space and more phones.

Finally at about noon, they arrived at the Police Academy, about a mile north of the firehouse. This was the place that was to be their headquarters for the next three days.

★CHAPTER SEVEN★

The mayor and his team kept on shuttling between the command post and Ground Zero, as it was already being called. They went once that afternoon, and three times that night. Fires were raging at the attack site, and at night the red, hellish glow could be seen from blocks away. Nobody knew how many thousands of people were buried under the rubble. Rudy and his aides did not speak to each other; what was there to say?

But he never stopped talking to the shaken, horrified people of New York City. People had spent the day, as they would for days to come, in front of their televisions, watching the videotapes of the planes hitting the towers, and the towers crumbling and falling, over and over and over again. Nobody even knew if it was all over, or if more attacks were on the way. It was like a bad dream from which the whole city, the whole country, could not be awakened. "It's going to be a very difficult time," the mayor said at a press conference that night. "I don't think we yet know the pain we're going to feel. But the thing we have to focus on now is getting the city through this and surviving and being stronger for it. New York is still here."

At about two thirty in the morning after the attack, Rudy finally went back to the apartment of the friends with whom he was staying. He was exhausted and still coated in the dust that had been the World Trade Center sixteen hours before. After hugging his friends, he lay down on his bed, keeping his boots beside him in case he had to leap up again. He turned on the television and watched the same awful replays of the disaster that everyone else had seen. Leaving the television on in case there was another attack, he finally opened the book he had been reading. It was a biography of the great English wartime leader, Winston Churchill. The British people will never forget his leadership and the rousing speeches that helped them feel that they would survive and even triumph, even as German bombs were dropping nightly on London. "I have nothing to offer," Churchill told his beleaguered people, "but blood, toil, tears, and sweat."

"I started thinking about Churchill," he told *Time*, "started thinking that we're going to have to rebuild the spirit of the city, and what better example than Churchill and the people of London during the Blitz in 1940, who had to keep up their spirit during this sustained bombing? It was a comforting thought."

And so, with Winston Churchill as his guide, Rudy spoke to the citizens of his city in a calm, rational voice. He did not lie. It was clear that he was feeling what everyone was feeling. But he was not giving in to despair or panic, and he was not going to let New Yorkers do it either. Although he himself had been through the terror of not knowing if he would survive, although he was learning constantly of people close to him who were lost, and although he was exhausted, he never faltered.

Meanwhile it was the president of the United States who was faltering. For a while he was simply missing in action; nobody knew where he was. It was ten hours before he would return to Washington. And when he did reemerge, he did not offer a reassuring presence. Eventually he would find his footing. But in those first days, he sounded, as the

New York Times said, "small and scripted."

Inevitably, the eyes of the entire country, and then the world, began to focus on Rudy Giuliani. The next week, the *Ottawa Citizen*, a Canadian newspaper, said, "It has been a week since a terrorist attack leveled the World Trade Center, and thanks largely to his uncanny ability to appear to be everywhere during this grim period, New York's mayor has risen from the ashes of the tragedy as an unequivocal hero of the moment."

Every day, the mayor stood before the cameras and gave us information, which was what everyone craved the most. How many people had been lost? A thousand? Five thousand? Twenty thousand? It was almost impossible to arrive at an accurate figure, and in fact it took weeks. But Rudy said that whatever the final total came to, "the number of casualties will be more than any of us can bear," and of course it was—2,843 souls were lost at Ground Zero. This number included 344 firefighters and Fire Department paramedics, along with scores of police officers and emergency rescue workers. Only five survivors were rescued alive after September 11. At the Pentagon, 234 people died, and 45 more on

United Flight 93, which crashed in Pennsylvania as its passengers thwarted an attempt to use the plane as a bomb at some other site. And the people who died were not just American: Eighty-six countries reported the loss of their citizens who had been working in the World Trade Center.

For days, the streets of downtown New York were filled with friends and relatives of the missing, who went from hospital to hospital, hoping against hope to find their loved ones. Every lamppost, every fence, was covered with homemade posters that showed photos of smiling people, along with identifying information about their birthmarks, rings, and tattoos. One of the first tasks Rudy's team had to accomplish was setting up a central place for these relatives to get information and help. It was set up at Saint Vincent's Hospital, the same one Rudy had passed the morning of the attacks on his way downtown.

There were a million other things to attend to, every minute of every day. When he was not at Ground Zero, Rudy was meeting with officials around a big table at the command center at the Police Academy. Each one reported in turn. How many trucks were removing debris from the site?

How many tons of concrete had been taken away? How many tons of steel? Where would they be taken so that the FBI could sift through every ounce of debris for evidence? Where would the search-and-rescue dogs and their handlers be housed? Which hospitals needed water? Where could people donate blood? Where could thousands of respirators be gotten in a hurry? Governor George Pataki sat in on these meetings, but he was just there to help; it was Rudy who made most of the decisions. People lined up to get answers to all these questions and thousands more. They were all urgent.

Rudy had a load of other headaches as well. The economy had already taken a nosedive in the last few months, as hundreds of Internet "dot-com" companies that had made the city pulse with excitement in the late 1990s had suddenly collapsed. And now everything had simply screeched to a halt. Businesses, stores, and restaurants downtown, even if they were unscathed physically, had zero clients. The tourist industry? Kaput. Nobody wanted to come to New York, and nobody wanted to fly. Rudy understood immediately that he would have to be a cheerleader for the local economy. "New York is open for business," he quickly started saying. He urged city dwellers to go out to eat and attend the theater, and urged out-of-towners to come to the Big Apple.

By this time, *New York* magazine was calling him the consoler-in-chief, even though the reality was that he himself was hurting as much as anybody else, perhaps more. He had lost so many friends. Almost the entire top leadership of the Fire Department perished in moments, and these were all people Rudy knew or had appointed. Beth Petrone-Hatton, who had been Rudy's personal assistant for eighteen years, lost her husband, Terry, a handsome Rescue One captain in the Fire Department. Rudy had performed their wedding in 1998.

As bodies of police and firefighters began to be recovered he started going to wakes and funerals. When a reporter asked him how many funerals he was attending, he said, "I try to get to three a day." And still he kept consoling the city, urging everyone to be strong and hopeful.

"I really do think that people should start thinking much more optimistically than they are," he said. "By that I mean, there's no question everybody is sad. We're mourning, we hurt, and we're going to hurt tomorrow, the next day, for a month, a year, and maybe forever. I think we are going to hurt forever. But we have to be optimistic. There's no reason for us not to be optimistic. All the same things about our economy are there that were there before. We have a big problem to overcome. But . . . I have no doubt the city is going to be economically stronger six months and a year from now."

Down at Ground Zero, the rescue operation continued day and night, as the entire city held its breath and hoped for someone to be pulled out of the still-burning rubble. But by September 25, that hope was fading. The mayor voiced what everyone was beginning to recognize. It would be a miracle, he said, if anyone were found alive. The rescue workers were not changing the definition of their mission, which was a search-and-rescue operation. But the city would begin helping relatives of the missing victims apply for death certificates.

And then, just when things were beginning to settle down—not to calmness, but at least to a jumpy sort of routine—there was the anthrax.

It started in Florida, with the death of a man who

worked at a tabloid newspaper there. It seemed like some sort of a weird fluke at first, though extremely troubling. The man had returned home from a fishing trip gravely ill, and it was discovered that he had inhaled a massive number of anthrax spores. Shortly afterward, a man who worked in the mailroom of the newspaper fell ill as well, though he miraculously escaped death.

Then the anthrax started showing up at the network news offices in New York. It came in letters, addressed in childish block letters, to news anchors Tom Brokaw and Peter Jennings. Brokaw's private secretary contracted the less-deadly skin form of anthrax when she handled the letter. At the offices of ABC television, a baby who had been brought in for an office party got infected. Then postal workers started falling ill from inhaled spores, as anthrax was discovered in the mail-processing areas of a local post office and also a facility in western New Jersey, where the letters had been mailed. Two of the postal workers died.

Then the anthrax letters turned up in Washington, in the office of Senator Tom Daschle. Over two dozen people who worked in his office were exposed to the powder in the letter, which was found to be incredibly potent and dangerous. The United States Capitol was shut down.

The country was freaking out. There were anthrax scares, anthrax threats, anthrax hoaxes, and evacuations of buildings every day, all over the country.

After anthrax spores were found in Governor Pataki's offices in New York, he and other members of his staff began taking Cipro, the powerful antibiotic known to be effective in combating the bacteria.

But Rudy was determined to keep everyone calm. Believing that panic would ultimately be much more harmful than the anthrax bacteria, he refused to take Cipro pills himself, against the advice of everyone around him. He appeared at press conferences, stayed relentlessly cheerful, and talked a lot about the Yankees. When he was pressed to talk about anthrax, he played it down. Because he was thinking a lot about Churchill and about the British who lived through the Blitz during World War II, he used their experience as an example. "So far," he told reporters, "this is all very, very psychological. We're not being bombed every day, like the people of London were bombed every day and still able to go on with their lives. So we can be just as brave as they were. This is easy, a lot easier than what they went through."

When somebody sneezed, he said, "Want to get checked? Only kidding," he added. "We've got to joke about this. It's the only way we're going to get through it."

There was no use pretending that everything was normal, though. "This is very uncharted territory that everybody is in," he remarked. But the message that he wanted to get across was the same one uttered by President Franklin D. Roosevelt during the Great Depression: "We have nothing to fear but fear itself."

Maybe fear was not okay, but sadness was unavoidable. Rudy cried in front of the television cameras at a promotion ceremony in late September, in which scores of Fire Department personnel were moved up to replace those who had died. "There was no way you could stand in that room and not cry," he told *Newsweek*.

And around that period, he felt an urge at about four o'clock in the morning to go down to Ground Zero by himself and just walk around. Realizing this would not be a good idea, he waited until it was daytime, and then he did it. It happened that while he was at the site, a firefighter was pulled out of the rubble. "It was just an unbelievable experience," he said. "The firefighters will not allow anyone else to extricate the bodies of their fallen brothers. They brought him down in between about forty firefighters who stood there, saluting, and then a priest came and gave a blessing. They carried him off. If you watch that and you don't cry, then you have to question whether you're human."

It was perhaps understandable, then, that Rudy, having lived through what he had lived through, did what he did when the Saudi prince came to town. Prince Alwaleed bin Talal bin Abdul Aziz Alsaud, a member of the fabulously wealthy royal family of Saudi Arabia, had long and close ties to the United States. Because of this, he wanted to come and see the devastation at the World Trade Center for himself. When he did, he was overwhelmed. He offered a ten-million-dollar check as a donation to the fund for the families of rescue workers who had been killed. But in a television interview, he also urged the United States to change its

Middle East policies. He felt that the U.S. was too sympathetic to the Israelis, and not enough to the Palestinians.

Rudy was outraged by this. In classic Rudy style, he did not discuss the disagreement with the prince. He simply refused the donation. Nobody was going to criticize his country after the barbarity of the World Trade Center attack. Even though ten million dollars would have been a lot of money for the surviving relatives, Rudy did not receive much criticism for his action. New York was behind Rudy all the way. Rudy was their guy.

In fact, Rudy was New York's guy to such an enormous degree that there began to be a lot of talk about an extended term for him. In the middle of everything else, the mayoral election was still going on. But many people felt that even though the mayor was not allowed by law to continue beyond the end of the year, there was really nobody else who could finish the job he had started. At first, Rudy brushed aside these suggestions. But gradually, he began to give them some consideration. He floated the idea that perhaps he could stay on for a while, if the city really needed him that much.

There was a tremendous amount of controversy about this development. Even though everyone agreed that Rudy had done a magnificent job through the crisis, it would have meant breaking the law to keep him on. And many people argued that if there was one thing that this country stands for, it is the rule of democratic law. If we threw away our own laws because of a crisis, some people reasoned, then the terrorists would have won a small victory. Opinion was split on the issue. One of the candidates, a Democrat, said that it would be okay with him to make way for Rudy to stay on for a few months. One of them said absolutely not.

In the end, Rudy backed out. He endorsed Michael Bloomberg, the Republican candidate, who had built a huge financial-media empire and had spent seventy-five million dollars of his own money on his campaign.

All he needed was Rudy's blessing. On election night, he came in first. He won by a small margin, but that was all he needed.

On New Year's Eve of 2001, Rudy pressed the button for the great glittering ball to drop in Times Square. Then, as he looked on smiling, Mike

Bloomberg was sworn in as New York's next mayor.

After January 1 Rudy Giuliani was a private citizen again. To reporters' questions about what he would do next, he had only vague replies. Maybe legal practice, maybe consulting. Of course, at this writing, nobody imagines that he is not thinking about politics anymore.

Of course, he is also still Rudy, and that means he was quickly embroiled in a number of fights. One was about a large fund of donated money for the survivors of the uniformed workers who died. After he was no longer mayor, he still felt he should control the fund, because he had personally raised a great deal of the money—and of course, being Rudy, he felt that he was the only person who could make the right decisions about how to distribute the money. But because he had a plan to hire about a dozen people to help administer the fund, and perhaps take months to distribute it, a group of widows took the issue to court. They wanted the fund to be under the official control of the City of New York. Finally Rudy caved in and agreed to give all the money out, right away.

Then there is the matter of the archives. Normally, when mayor of New York leaves office, his papers go to the official New York City archives, where they are catalogued by archivists so that scholars and journalists can use them for research. But Rudy, again being Rudy, decided he wanted more control over his papers. So he made a last-minute deal before he left office to hold on to them, and hire his own archivists to sort them. This, of course, raised the delicate question of whether certain documents would never see the light of day, which is of course vigorously denied by Rudy's archivists. It promises to be a long, drawn-out fight.

Or should we call him Sir Rudy? In February, Rudy, his former Fire Commissioner Thomas Von Essen, and former Police Commissioner Bernard Kerik traveled to Buckingham Palace in England. There, in a stately ceremony, Rudy received an honorary knighthood from Queen Elizabeth II. Von Essen and Kerik were made honorary Commanders of the British Empire. Rudy got two medals: a blue-and-red enameled cross on a red ribbon, and the Star of the Knight Commander, a jewel-encrusted silver star, which he dedicated to the people of New

York. Only British subjects are allowed to kneel and have a sword touched to each shoulder, so Rudy didn't do that. But he did bow to the Queen. "I told her," he told the *New York Times*, "that I believe I speak for all the people of New York and America in thanking her for the tremendous support after September 11. We need friends and we have no better friends than Great Britain."

Actually, we are not allowed to call him "Sir Rudy." Honorary knights do not use that title. Besides, said Rudy, "They won't call me that in Brooklyn."

★ ★ ★

It is too soon to know how history will finally judge Rudy Giuliani. It takes a while for a political leader's legacy to gel in the minds of the public, and Rudy's legacy is an extraordinary mixture of highs and lows. But it is safe to say that the Rudy we got to know on September 11 and afterward will not be forgotten, ever.

One thing is certain: whatever Rudy has done, at every point in his career, he did because he was sure he was right, for better or for worse. He was always *real*, not for one minute an airbrushed politician who didn't make a move without advice from media consultants and pollsters. Rudy did not much care about polls.

One thing he always cared about was the lessons he had received from his father. And if there was ever a moment for Rudy to use those lessons, the morning of September 11 was that moment. Harold Giuliani, a flawed man who had been battered and frustrated by life, wanted desperately for his son to grow up straight and tall. He wanted Rudy to be a beacon of uncompromising morality. He spent a huge amount of his energy in trying to pass on what he had learned through hard experience. He wanted to keep Rudy from falling prey to the same traps that life, or his own personality, had seemed always to set for him. The final conversation they had before Harold's death from prostate cancer, Rudy recalled, "was about courage and fear. I said to him, 'Were you ever afraid of anything?' He said to me, 'Always.' He said, 'Courage is being afraid but then doing what you have to do anyway.'"

At one of the many funerals Rudy Giuliani attended after September 11, he spoke again about courage. "It is the quality which guarantees all others," he said. "Without courage, nothing else can happen."

The whole world had seen the mayor of New York—the mayor of the world for a moment—demonstrating the truth of this statement since that horrific day. Rudy Giuliani, in all his argumentative, frustrating, stubborn, opinionated glory, had lent his courage to us all, and we were lucky to have it.

Read another exciting
political biography from
Aladdin Paperbacks

INCLUDES
COVERAGE OF
THE HISTORIC
2000
ELECTION!

PRESIDENT
GEORGE W. BUSH
Our Forty-third President

Beatrice Gormley